THIS WALKER BOOK BELONGS TO:

For Johanna
M.W.

For Leon
"Magic with Flowers"
C.A.

First published 1999 by Walker Books Ltd
87 Vauxhall Walk, London SE11 5HJ

This edition published 2000

2 4 6 8 10 9 7 5 3 1

This book has been typeset in Granjon.

Printed in Hong Kong

British Library Cataloguing in Publication Data
A catalogue record for this book is available from the British Library.

ISBN 0-7445-7742-X

WHO DO YOU LOVE?

Martin Waddell

Illustrated by Camilla Ashforth

WALKER BOOKS
AND SUBSIDIARIES
LONDON · BOSTON · SYDNEY

Holly played on the hillside
each night, until Mama
called her in for her tea.
"Night-night!" Holly said.
"Night-night, Holly!" called her
friends and Holly went in.

"Bedtime now, Holly!" said Mama,
when they had finished their tea.
"I want to play our go-to-bed
game!" Holly said.
"Bed first, then the game,"
Mama said.
"I want to play while I'm getting
ready for bed," Holly said.
And Mama started the game.

"Who do you love, Holly?"
asked Mama.

"I love Grandpa," Holly said.

"He takes me for walks in the wood
and he makes dandelion clocks
for me. And I hide away where he
can't see me. He says, 'Where are
you, Holly?' Then I jump out
and shout **BOO!**"

"Poor Grandpa!" said Mama.

"Now ask me again!" Holly said.

"Who do you love?" asked Mama.

"Let me think!" Holly said.

"I love Grandma because she makes
big cakes at her house. She stirs the
mix and I put the cherries on top.
Then I lick the spoon. Grandma
makes the best cakes in the wood."

"You'll get fat eating cakes,"
said Mama.

"I don't care!" Holly said. "I like
Grandma's cakes."

Mama looked for the towel but Holly
wanted more of the game.

"Ask me who I love," Holly said.

"Ask me again!"

"Who do you love?" asked Mama.

"I love Arthur," said Holly.

"I love Arthur because he is my brother. He lets me ride on his bike. Sometimes I ride down the hill and then I fall off in the grass at the bottom. Arthur says that's how you learn to ride bikes."

"I see!" said Mama.

"Ask me some more!"
Holly said.

"Who do you love?" asked Mama.

"I love Pa because he is my Pa,"
Holly said. "He tells me stories all
about my adventures."

"What sort of adventures?"
asked Mama.

"I was a princess and I lived
in a castle with Arthur. One day
there was a dragon and Arthur didn't
know what to do. I got some water
and poured it all over the dragon
and put his fire out. Pa says I saved
Arthur, and I made the dragon
my friend," Holly said.

"Who else do you love?"
 asked Mama.
"I think I've done everyone now,"
 Holly said.
"You've left someone out!"
 said Mama.
 It was the part of the game that
 Holly liked best.
"Ask me again!" Holly said.
"Who do you love, Holly?"
 asked Mama.

"I love ... old Postman
Cat because he brings us
our letters," Holly said.
"Just old Postman Cat?"
asked Mama.

"I love ...
Cousin Ollie
who comes every
Sunday," Holly said.
"I love Cousin Ollie a lot!"

"I love ...
the cat with the hat
that we met yesterday
in the wood,"
Holly said.

"I love ...
the three kittens
who roll down
the hill,"
Holly said.

"I think I might cry!" sighed Mama.

"Don't cry, Mama," Holly said.

"You just have to ask me again."

"Who do you love, Holly?"
 asked Mama.

"I love you," said Holly.

"And I love you too," Mama said.

"You know that I do."

Mama hugged Holly and put her to bed,

and that was the end of the

go-to-bed game.

WALKER 🐻 BOOKS

Who Do You Love?

MARTIN WADDELL says that *Who Do You Love?*, like all of his picture book stories, was "written for that special island of time at the end of the day. My books are for parents and children to share."

Martin Waddell is the distinguished author of over one hundred children's books. He has won the Smarties Book Prize twice – for *Can't You Sleep, Little Bear?* and *Farmer Duck* – as well as the Best Books for Babies Award for *Rosie's Babies* and the Kurt Maschler Award for *The Park in the Dark*. Martin lives with his wife Rosaleen in Newcastle, County Down.

CAMILLA ASHFORTH says, "It was lovely illustrating *Who Do You Love?*, as it's a game all three of my children have teased me with since they were tiny."

Camilla Ashforth is the author and illustrator of the James and Horatio books: *Horatio's Bed*, *Monkey Tricks*, *Calamity* and *Humphrey Thud*. She has also designed theatre sets and costumes and has exhibited her watercolour paintings. Camilla lives in London with her children.

ISBN 0-7445-3156-X (pb)

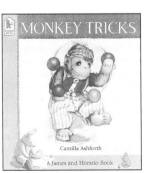

ISBN 0-7445-3168-3 (pb)

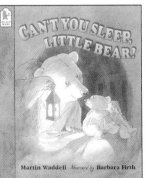

ISBN 0-7445-7294-0 (pb)

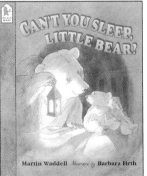

ISBN 0-7445-2335-4 (pb)